My Little Foster Sister

Muriel Stanek • *Illustrated by* Judith Cheng

Albert Whitman & Company, Chicago

Library of Congress Cataloging in Publication Data

Stanek, Muriel.
 My little foster sister.

 (Concept books: Level 1)
 Summary: An only child first rejects and then
grows to accept and love her foster sister.
 [1. Foster home care—Fiction. 2. Brothers and
sisters—Fiction] I. Cheng, Judith, ill. II. Title.
III. Series.
PZ7.S78637My   [E]   81-13006
ISBN 0-8075-5365-4   AACR2

The text of this book is set in 16/22 Fairfield.

To the Sieger family
and their foster children

One day Penny came to live with us.
She was a foster child.

Mama said that Penny's parents had died.
"She'll stay here with us until someone
adopts her," Mama told me. "We're going to
be her family—but just for a while."

Daddy said we should be kind to Penny.
"She's very shy and a little frightened."

"But she doesn't belong here!" I told them.

On Penny's first night with us, she sat
in my chair at dinner. I told her to move.
"That's my place," I said. "And don't forget it!"

I put a sign on my bedroom door. "Keep out,"
I told her. "Remember that!"

When Daddy and I went shopping at the
supermarket, we had to take Penny along.
She sat in the cart, and I had to help push.

Mama said I should give Penny some of my old toys. "They're mine," I told her. "And I don't want any little kid breaking them."

But Mama said I had to give Penny some toys anyway.

When Granny came to visit, she let Penny
sit on her lap and hold her purse.

"But Granny's MY grandmother," I said
to myself.

One day Mama gave Penny my red sweater. "But that's my favorite sweater with the kitten on it!" I cried.

"You've outgrown it," Mama said. "And Penny needs a sweater."

When Mama was painting the kitchen, she asked me to take Penny to the playground.

"Do I have to take her?" I asked.

Mama said, "Yes! You both need some fresh air. And don't forget to look out for Penny."

I put Penny on the bench and told her to
stay there while I played ball.

While I was at bat, Penny walked over
to the slide. "She's old enough to go
on the slide by herself," I thought.

But a big boy came and pushed her down just as she was starting to climb the ladder.

I ran over there and said, "What's the
big idea of pushing a little girl?"

"What do you care?" the boy yelled. "It's
none of your business."

"It IS my business, you big bully," I
yelled back. "She's . . . she's my foster sister,
and I'm here to see that she gets her turn."

Then the big bully backed away and ran toward
the fence. Penny went down the slide all by
herself. And I caught her at the bottom.

I think she had a good time at the playground.
On the way home, she held my hand tightly.

Penny was too little to go to school. But
each day when I came home, she was waiting
for me at the window. Sometimes she hid behind
the door and said, "Boo!" as I walked in. Then
she'd laugh when I pretended to look surprised.

Penny liked having me read *Peter Rabbit* to
her. She always said the names of the little
rabbits, "Flopsy, Mopsy, Cotton Tail,
and Peter."

I showed her how I practice my piano lessons.
And she sang "Twinkle, Twinkle, Little Star,"
while I played it.

One night a terrible storm woke me up. A flash of lightning lit up my room for a moment. There standing by my bed was Penny. She looked like a tiny ghost in her long, white nightgown.

"Are you scared?" I asked.

She nodded, and I threw back the covers. "Climb in," I said. She snuggled up next to me, and I put my arm around her.

The next day I took the keep-out sign off
my door.

I told Penny she could play with
all my toys while I was at school.

One night Mama and Daddy looked sad. "Penny will be leaving us soon," Mama said. "She's being adopted by her aunt and uncle in California."

"Can't she stay with us anymore?" I asked.

"No," said Daddy. "I wish she could. But her aunt and uncle want her very much. They don't have any children of their own."

Mama said, "Penny won't be a foster child anymore. She'll have a family and a home all her own."

I gave Penny my *Peter Rabbit* book on the day she left.

And Daddy took our picture together.

When we hugged for the last time,
Penny didn't want to let go of me.

I cried as she drove away with her
new family.

I miss seeing Penny at the window when
I come home from school every day. And I
miss taking her to the playground.

It was nice having a foster sister,
even for a little while.